What to do:

1 Roll the A2 card (you can also use an 18in x 24in sheet of black construction paper) into a cone shape.

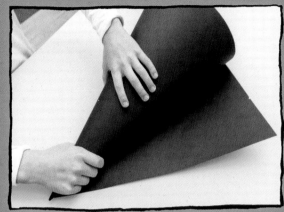

2 Fit the cone on your head and ask a friend to stick tape down the long edge to secure. Trim the bottom of the cone so it's even all the way around.

3 Draw as large of a circle as you can on the A3 card (you can also use a 12in x 18in sheet of black construction paper) and cut it out.

4 Place the cone in the middle of the circle and draw around it with a pencil.

5 Remove the cone t[...] Now draw a smalle[...] first circle and cut it out.

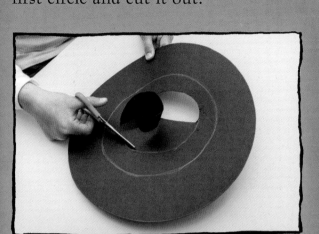

6 Cut flaps from the inside circle to the pencil circle. Place the cone on top and bend the flaps up inside it, then stick them down firmly with tape.

You can lay out lots of things to decorate your hats, like stickers, paint, pens, pompoms, foam shapes, or collage material. Don't forget glue so you can stick them on!

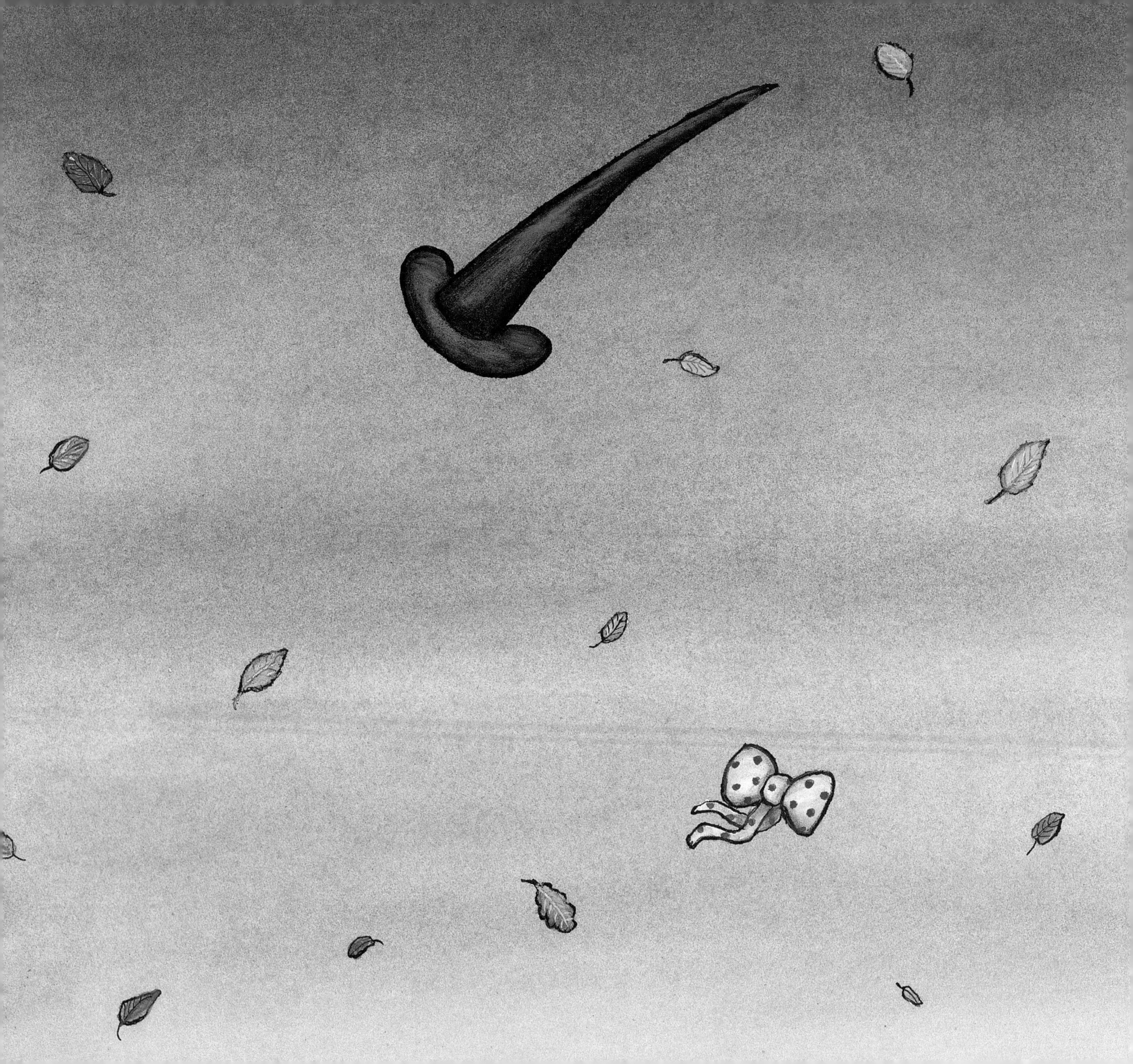

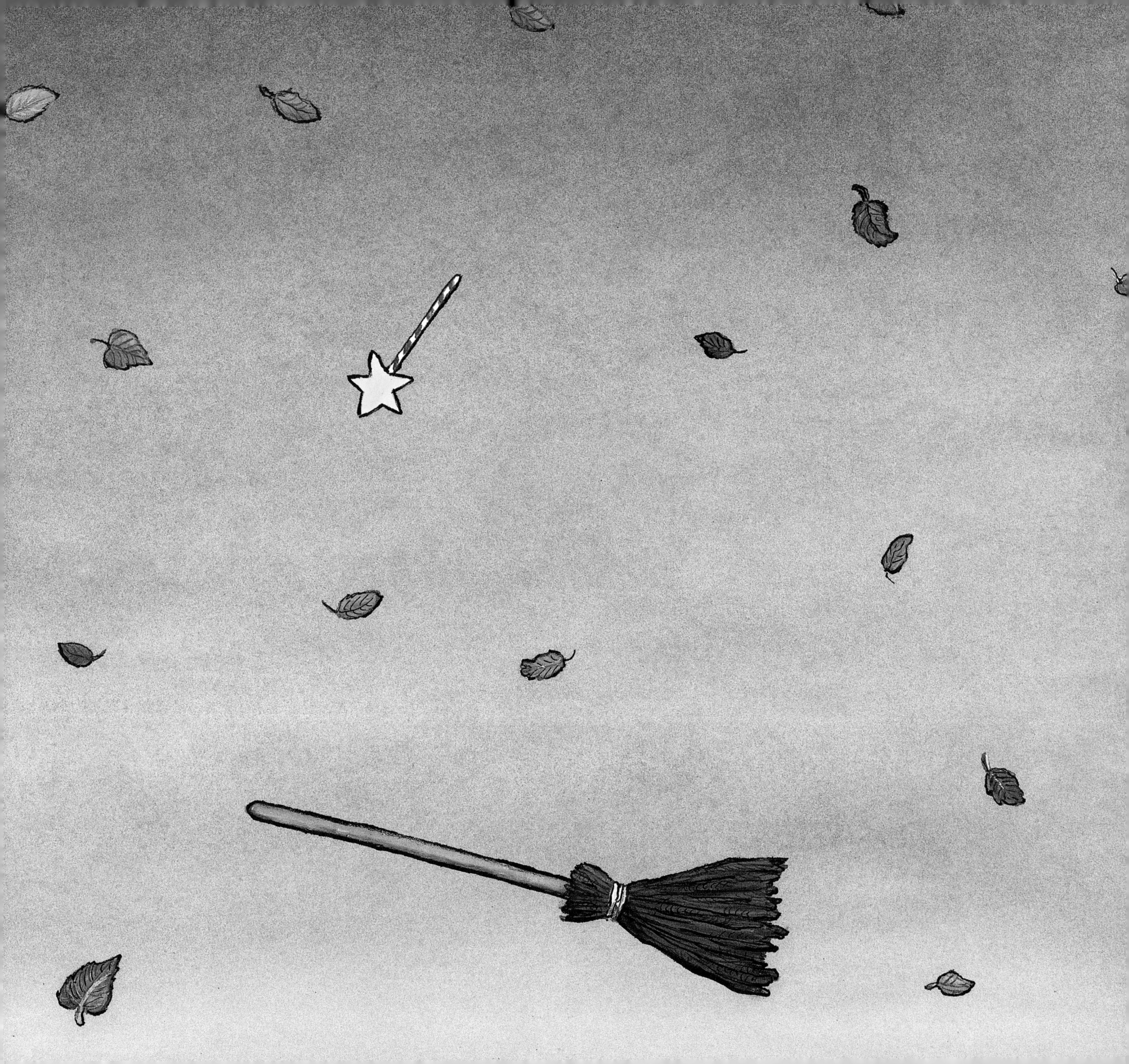

For Natasha, Sabrina and Jasmine – J.D.

Dial Books for Young Readers
An imprint of Penguin Random House LLC
1745 Broadway, New York, New York 10019

First published by Macmillan Children's Books, 2001
This edition first published in the United Kingdom by Macmillan Children's Books, an imprint of Pan Macmillan, 2023
This edition first published in the United States of America by Dial Books for Young Readers, an imprint of Penguin Random House LLC, 2024

Text copyright © 2001, 2024 by Julia Donaldson
Illustrations copyright © 2001, 2024 by Axel Scheffler

Visit us online at PenguinRandomHouse.com.

THE LIBRARY OF CONGRESS HAS CATALOGED THE DIAL EDITION AS FOLLOWS:
Donaldson, Julia. Room on the broom / by Julia Donaldson ; pictures by Axel Scheffler. p. cm.
Summary: A witch finds room on her broom for all the animals that ask for a ride, and they repay her kindness by rescuing her from a dragon.
ISBN: 0-8037-2657-0 (hc)
[1. Witches—Fiction. 2. Animals—Fiction. 3. Dragons—Fiction. 4. Stories in rhyme.]
1. Scheffler, Axel, ill. II. Title. PZ8.3.D7234 Ro 2001 [E]—dc21 00-045182

ISBN 9780593859926

1 2 3 4 5 6 7 8 9 10

Manufactured in China

Text set in Bernhard Modern

Room on the Broom

by Julia Donaldson

pictures by Axel Scheffler

DIAL BOOKS FOR YOUNG READERS NEW YORK

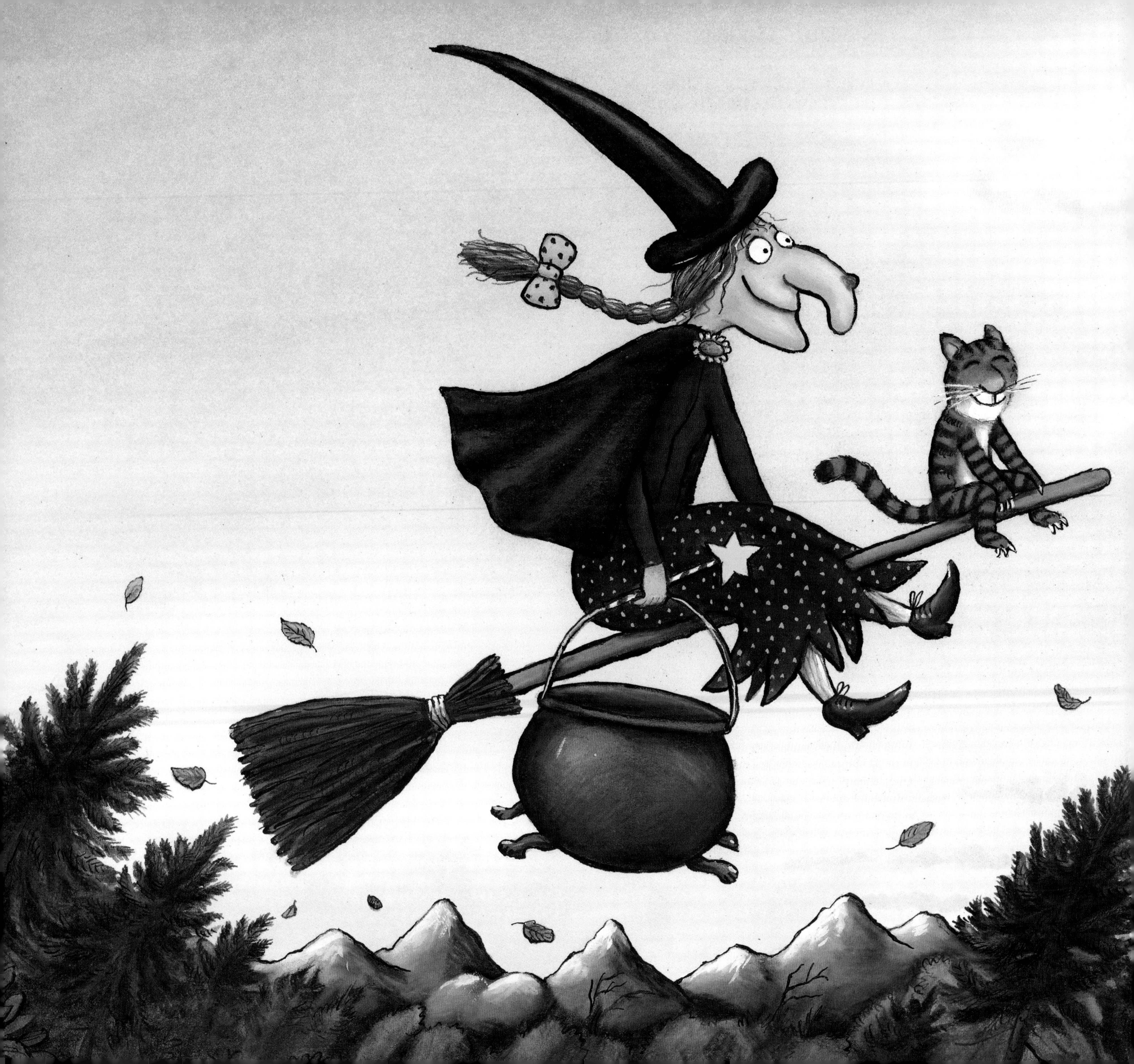

The witch had a cat
    and a hat that was black,
And long ginger hair
    in a braid down her back.
How the cat purred
    and how the witch grinned,
As they sat on their broomstick
    and flew through the wind.

But how the witch wailed
    and how the cat spat,
When the wind blew so wildly,
    it blew off the hat.

"Down!" cried the witch,
    and they flew to the ground.
They searched for the hat,
    but no hat could be found.

Then out of the bushes
    on thundering paws
There bounded a dog
    with the hat in his jaws.

He dropped it politely,
then eagerly said
(As the witch pulled the hat
firmly down on her head),
"I am a dog, as keen as can be.
Is there room on the broom
for a dog like me?"

"Yes!" cried the witch,
and the dog clambered on.
The witch tapped the broomstick and
whoosh! they were gone.

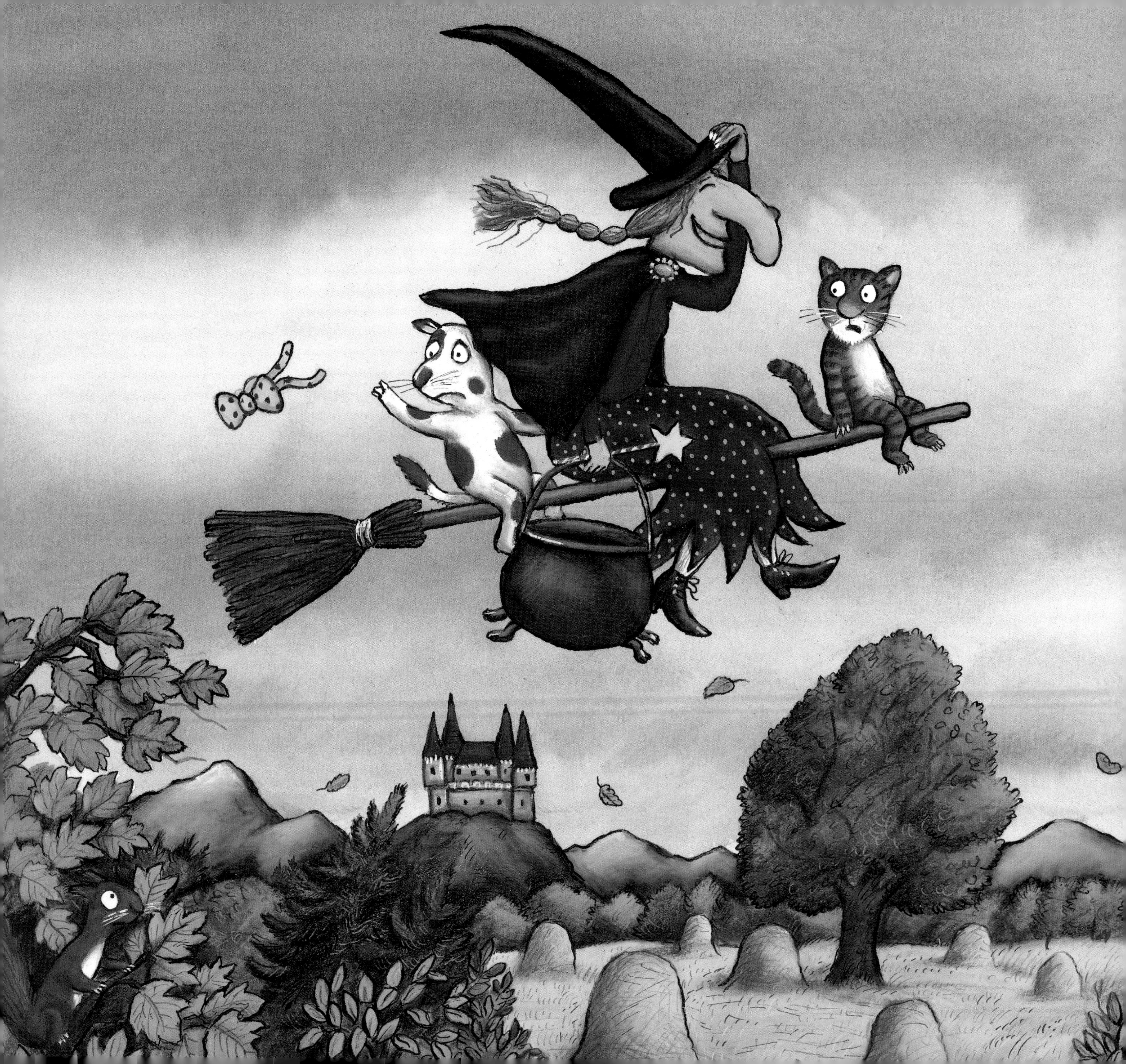

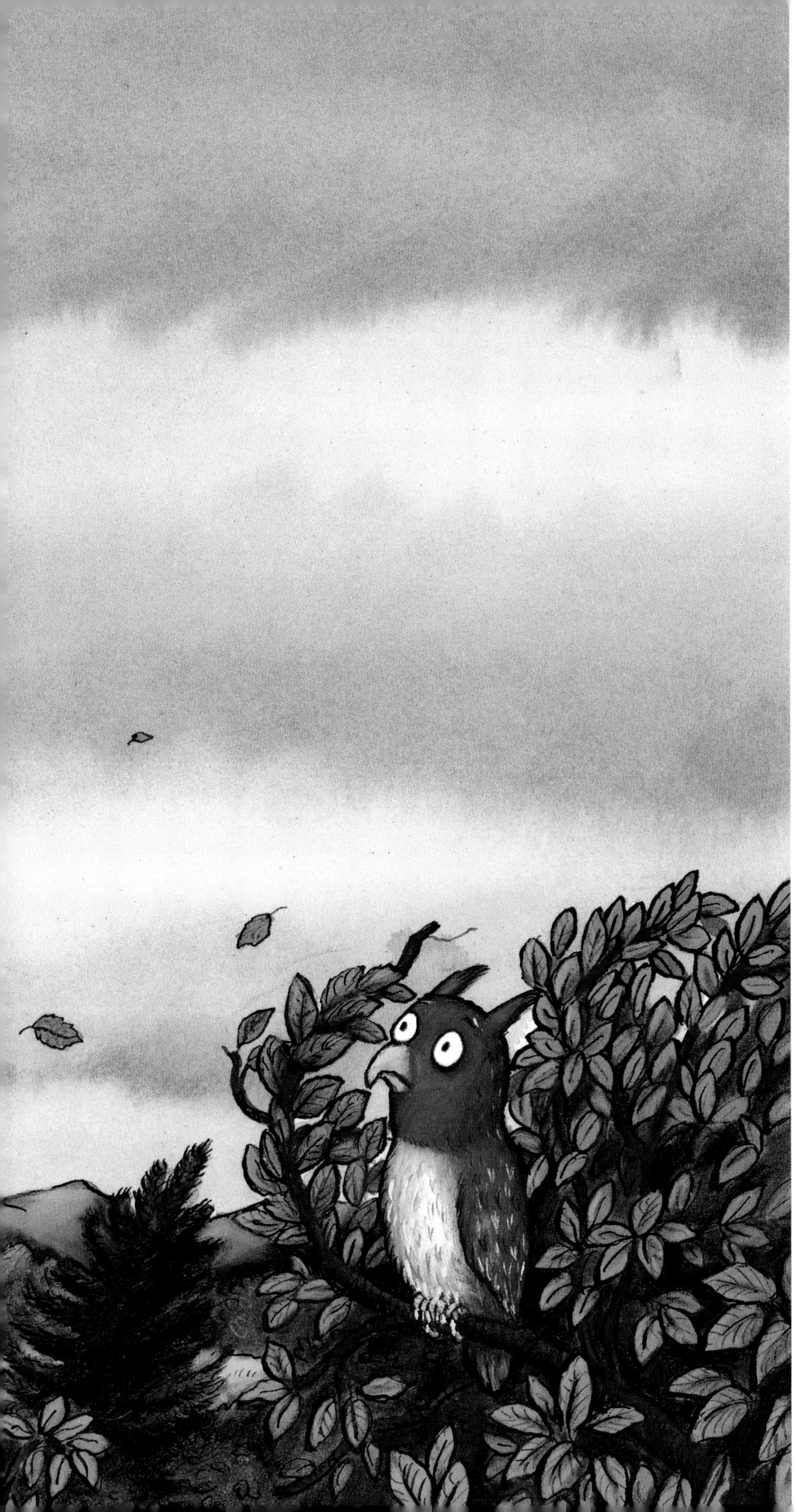

Over the fields and the
forests they flew.
The dog wagged his tail
and the stormy wind blew.
The witch laughed out loud
and held on to her hat,
But away blew the bow
from her braid—just like that!

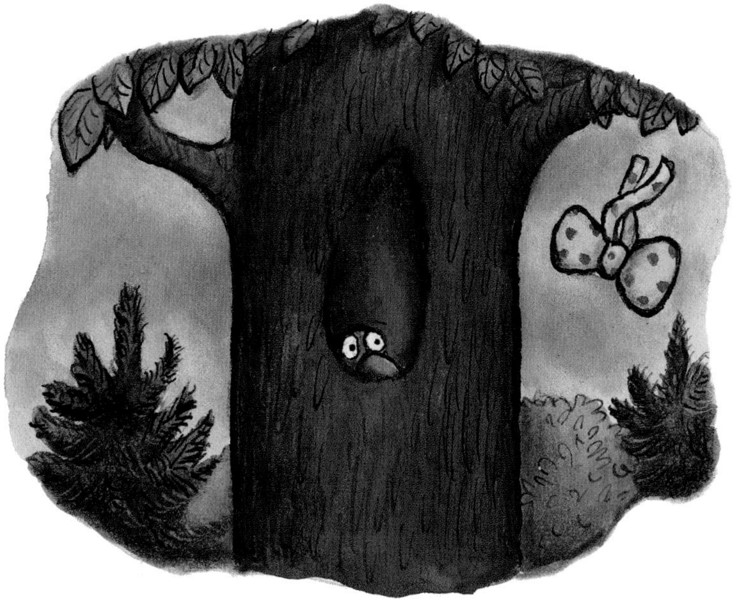

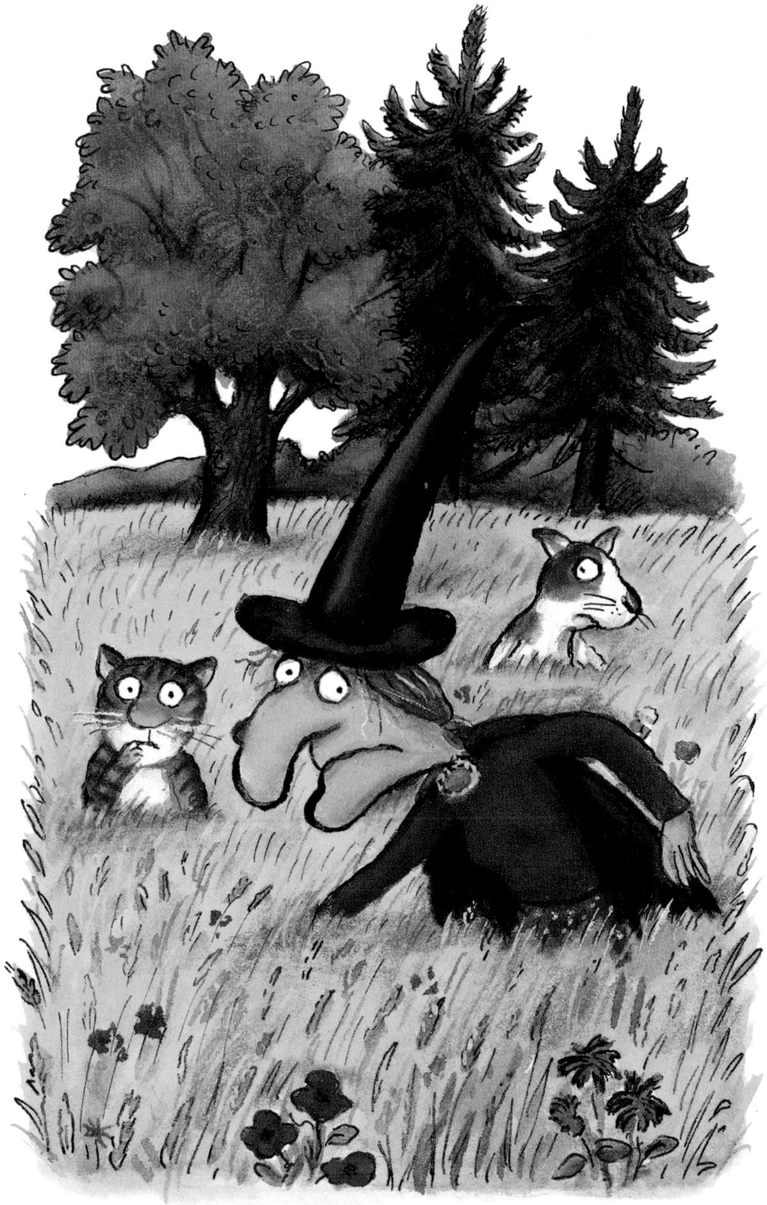

"Down!" cried the witch,
and they flew to the ground.
They searched for the bow,
but no bow could be found.

Then out from a tree,
with an ear-splitting shriek,
There flapped a green bird
with the bow in her beak.
She dropped it politely
and bent her head low,

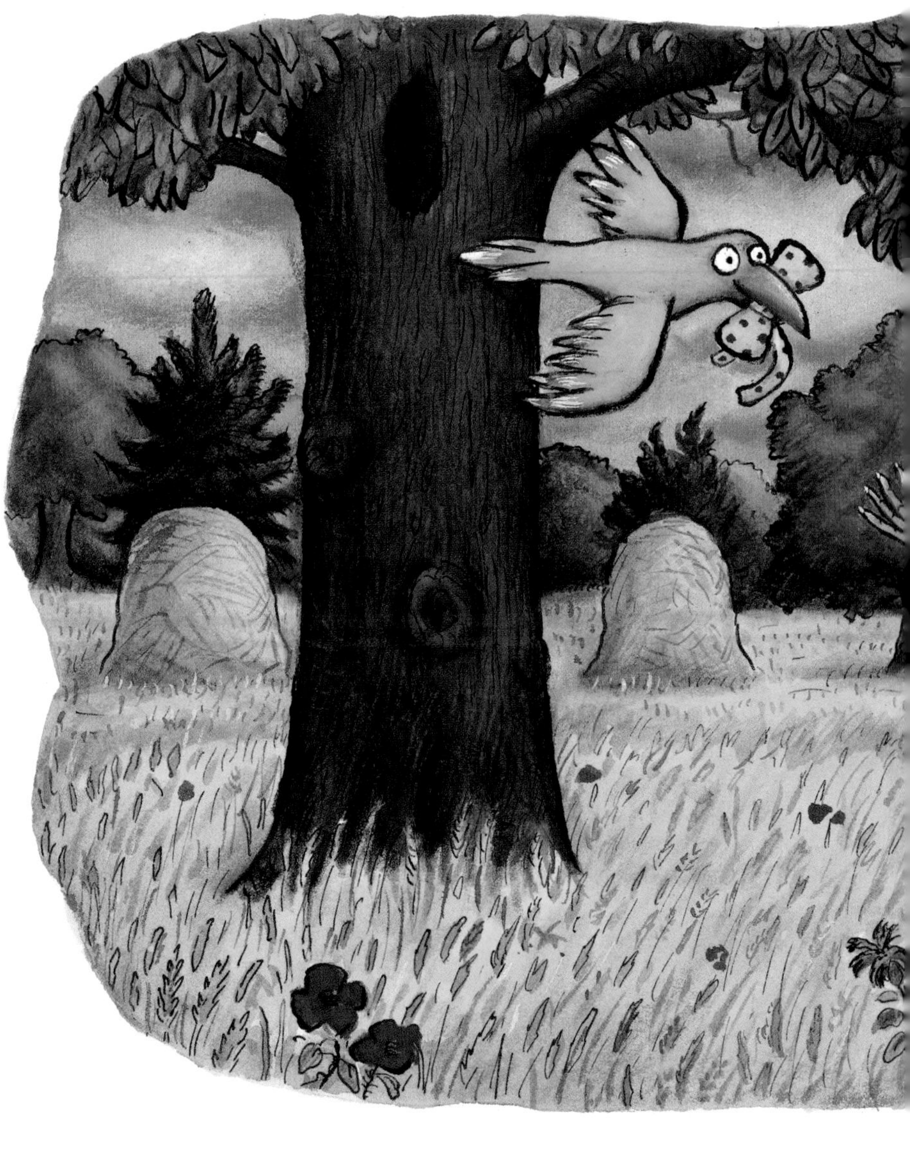

Then said (as the witch
tied her braid in the bow),
"I am a bird,
as green as can be.
Is there room on the broom
for a bird like me?"

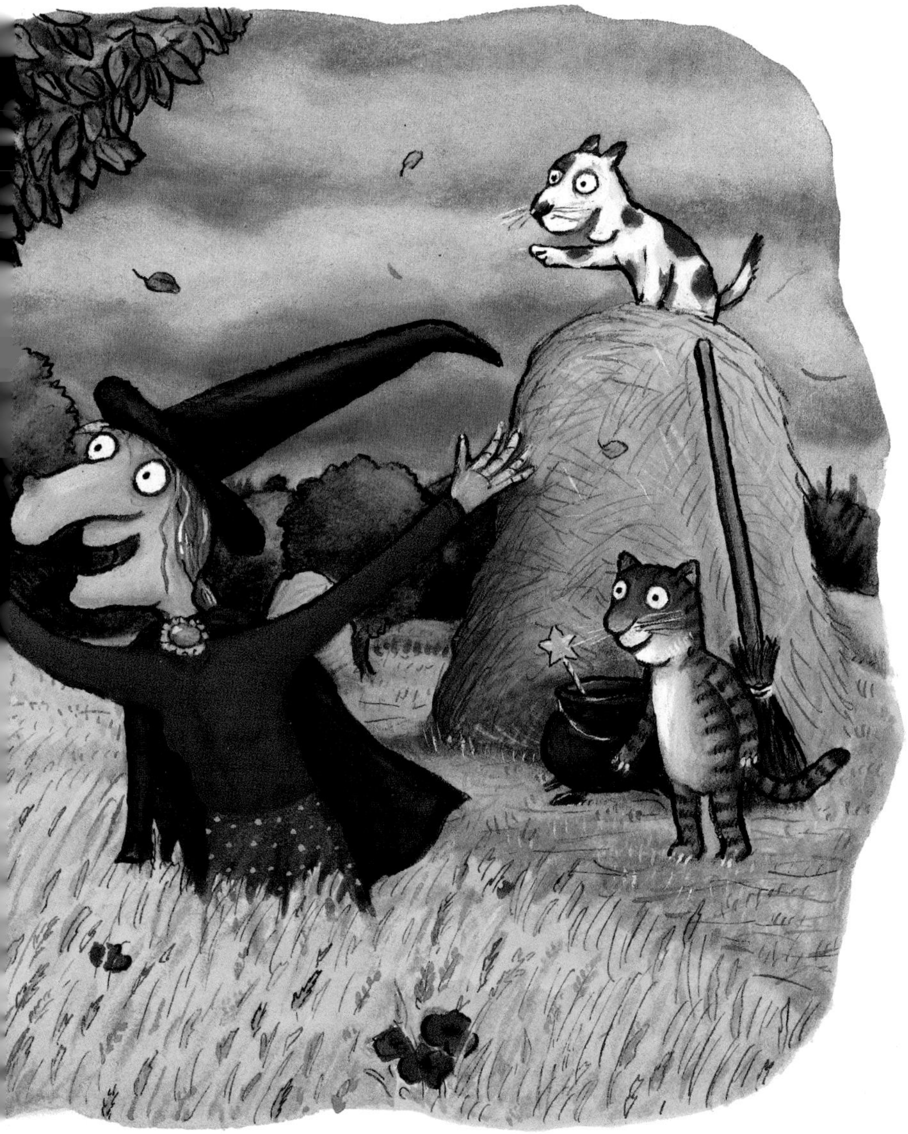

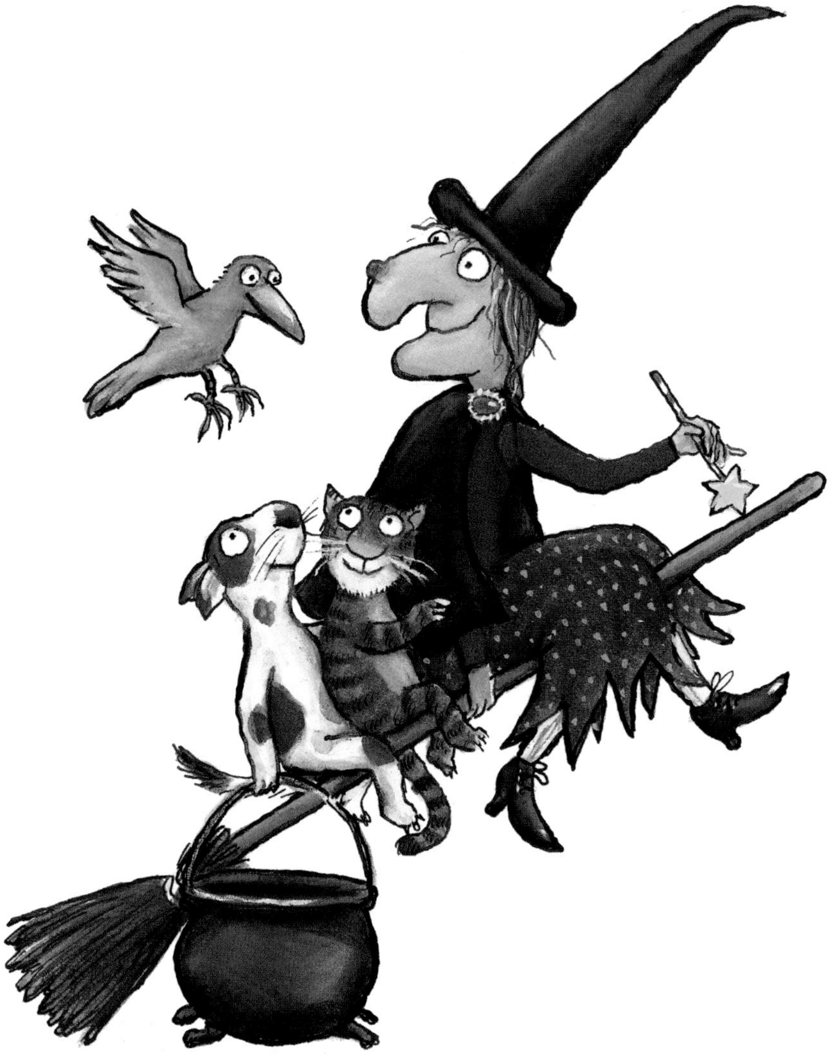

"Yes!" cried the witch,
so the bird fluttered on.
The witch tapped the broomstick and
whoosh! they were gone.

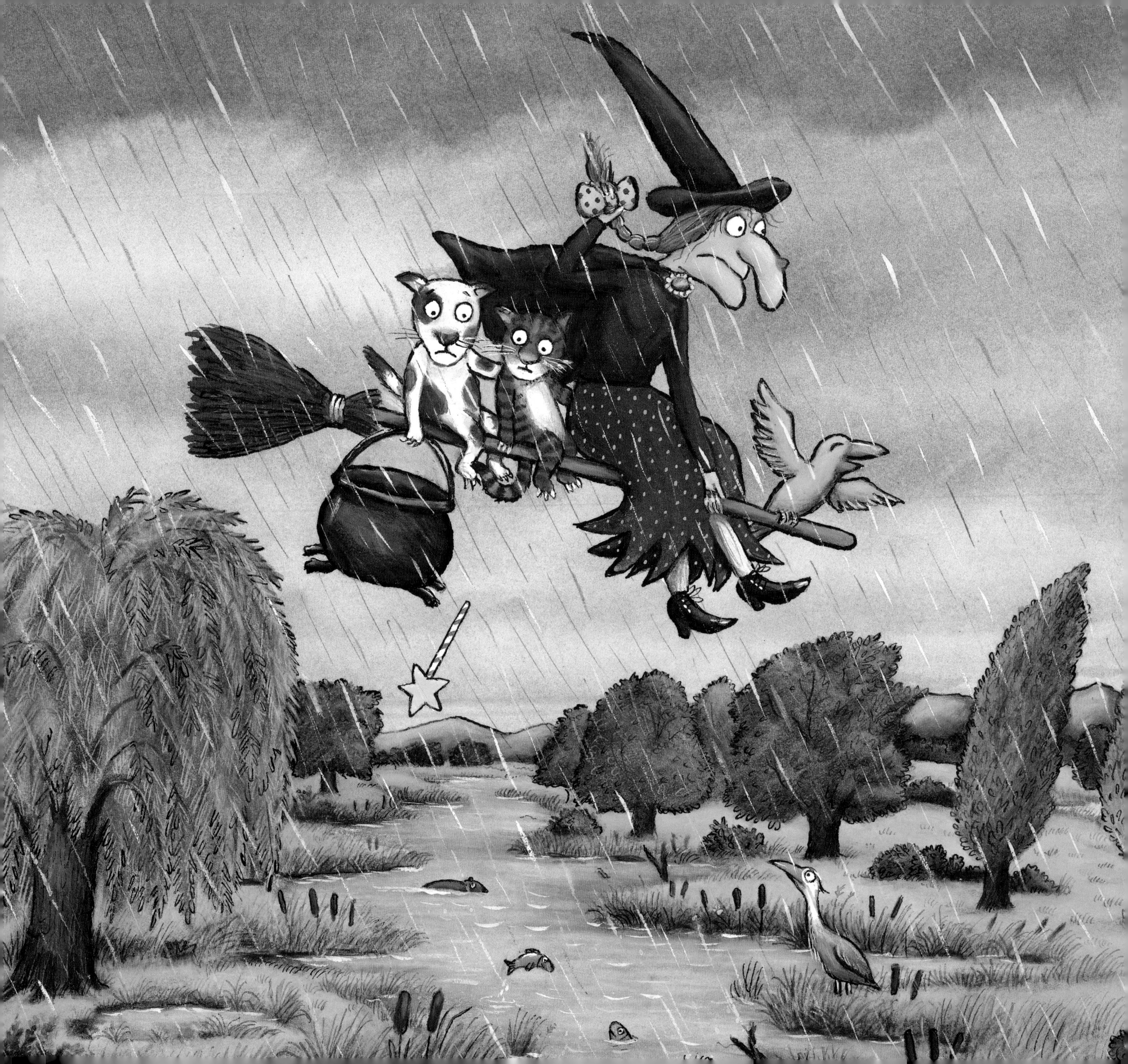

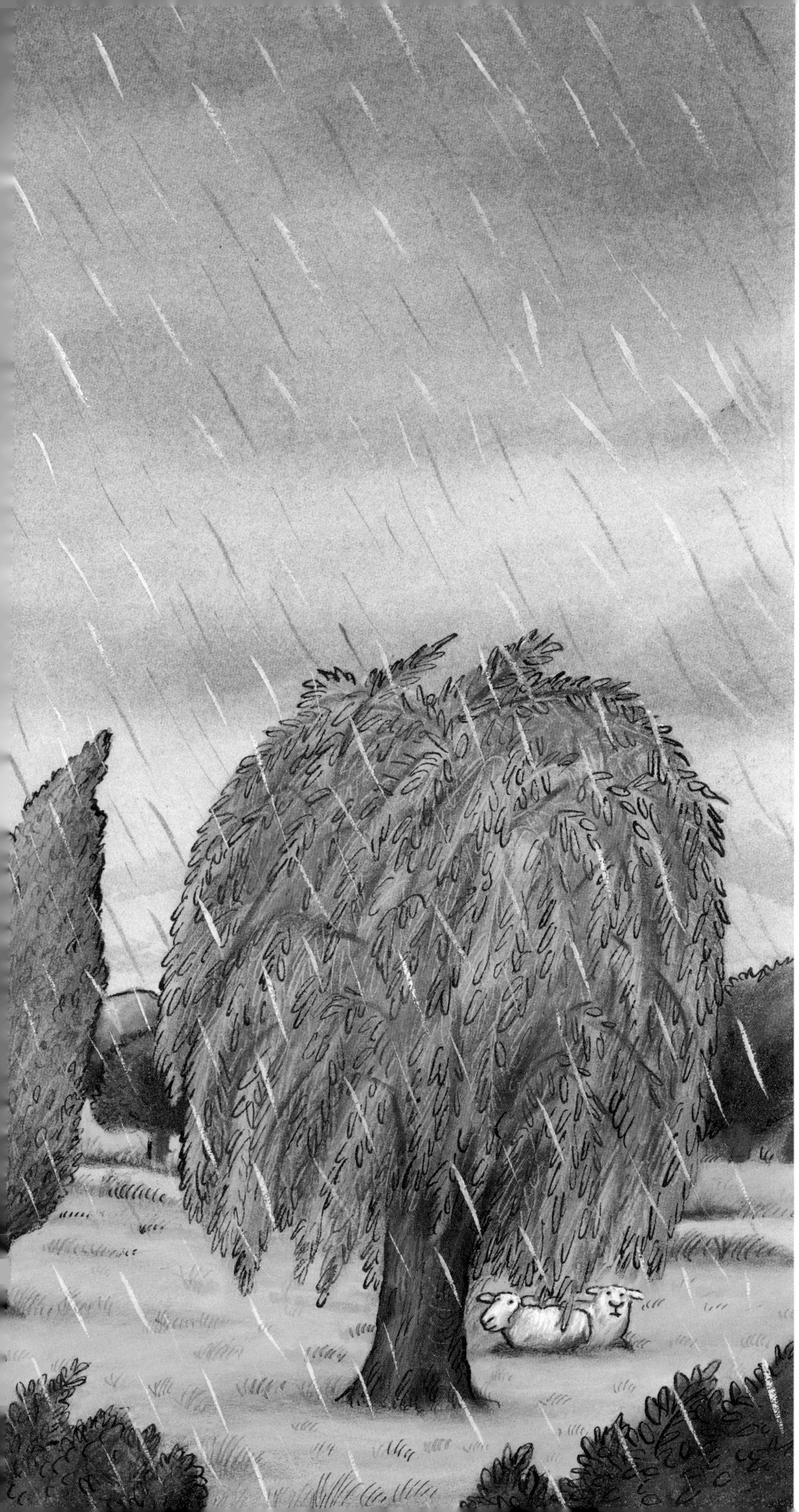

Over the reeds and the
rivers they flew.
The bird shrieked with glee
and the stormy wind blew.
They shot through the sky
to the back of beyond.
The witch clutched her bow—
but let go of her wand.

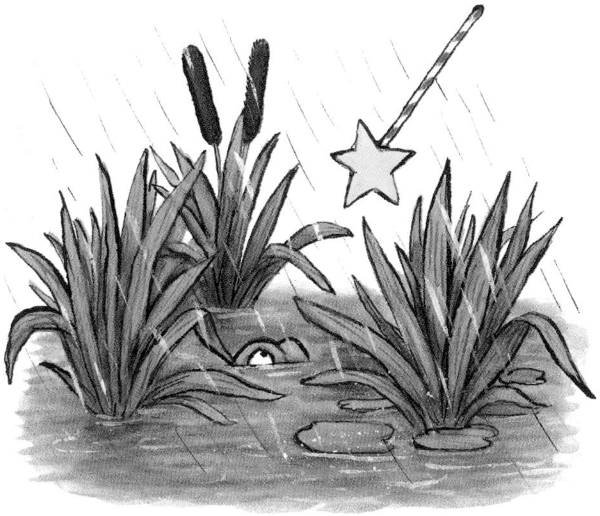

"Down!" cried the witch,
and they flew to the ground.
They searched for the wand,
but no wand could be found.

Then all of a sudden
   from out of a pond
Leaped a dripping wet frog
   with a dripping wet wand.
He dropped it politely,
   then said with a croak
(As the witch dried the wand
   on a fold of her cloak),
"I am a frog, as clean as can be.
Is there room on the broom
   for a frog like me?"
"Yes!" said the witch, so the frog
   bounded on.

The witch tapped the broomstick and
   whoosh! they were gone.
Over the moors and the
   mountains they flew.
The frog jumped for joy and . . .

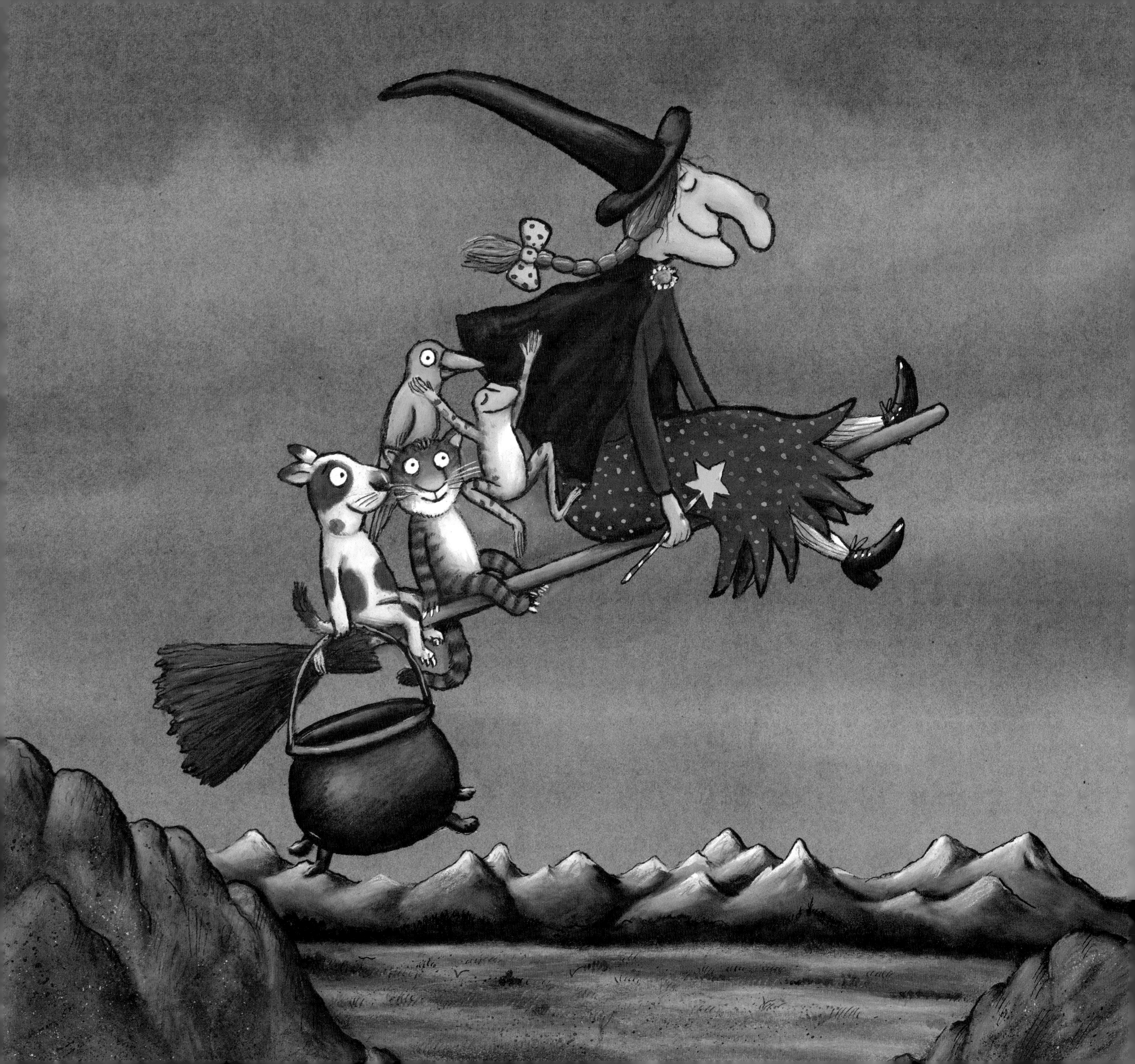

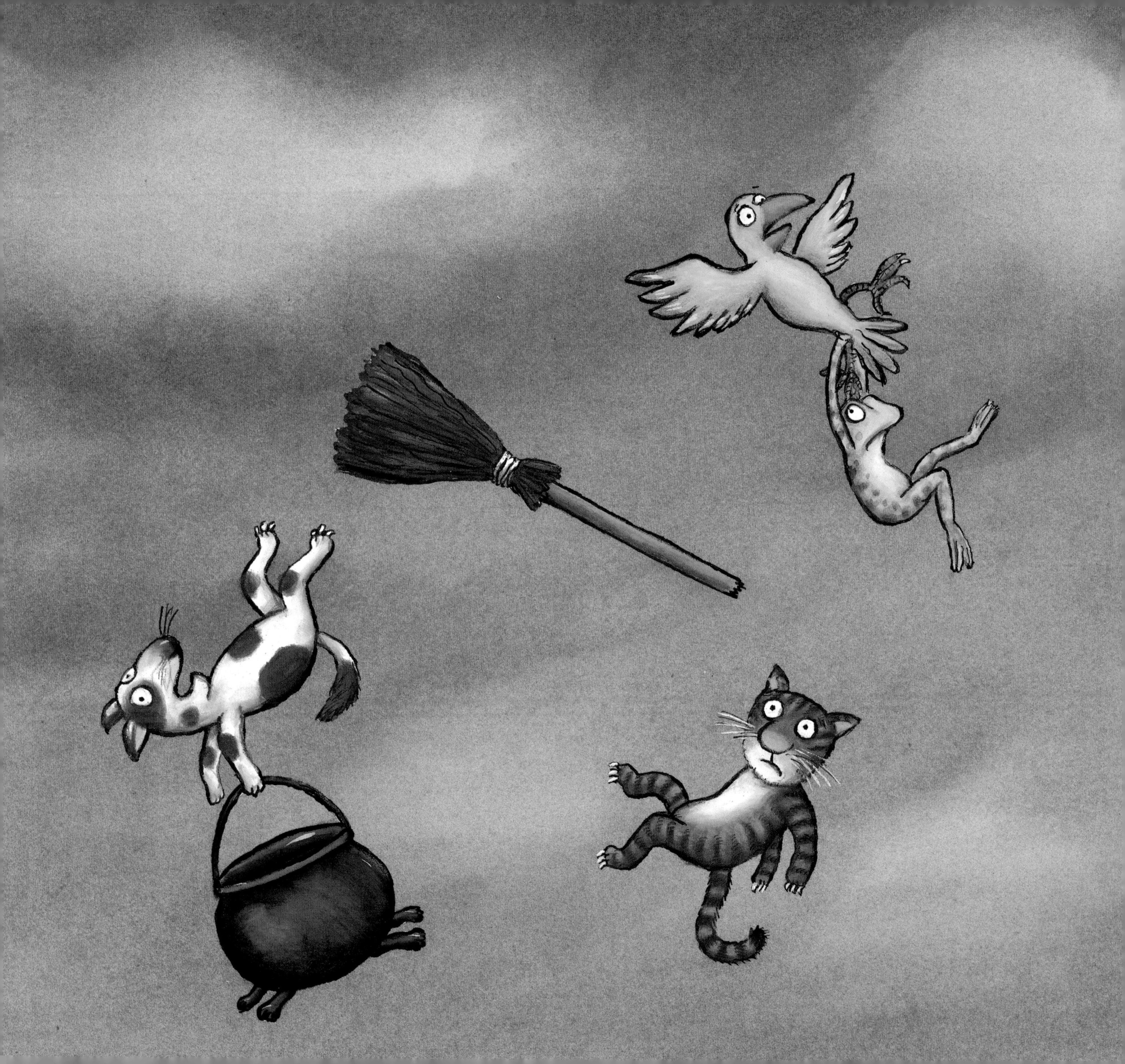

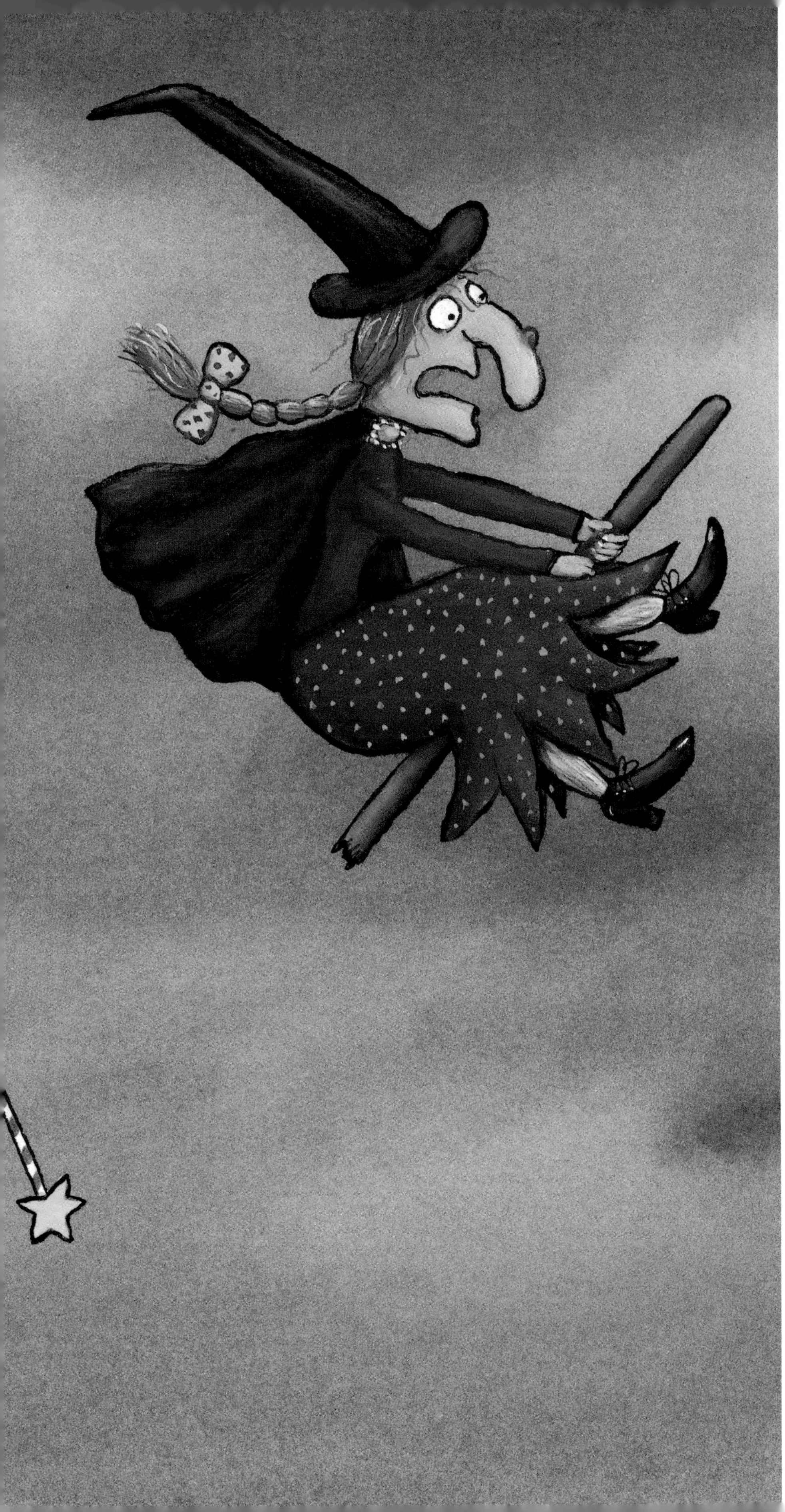

THE BROOM SNAPPED IN TWO!

Down fell the cat and the dog
and the frog.
Down they went tumbling
into a bog.

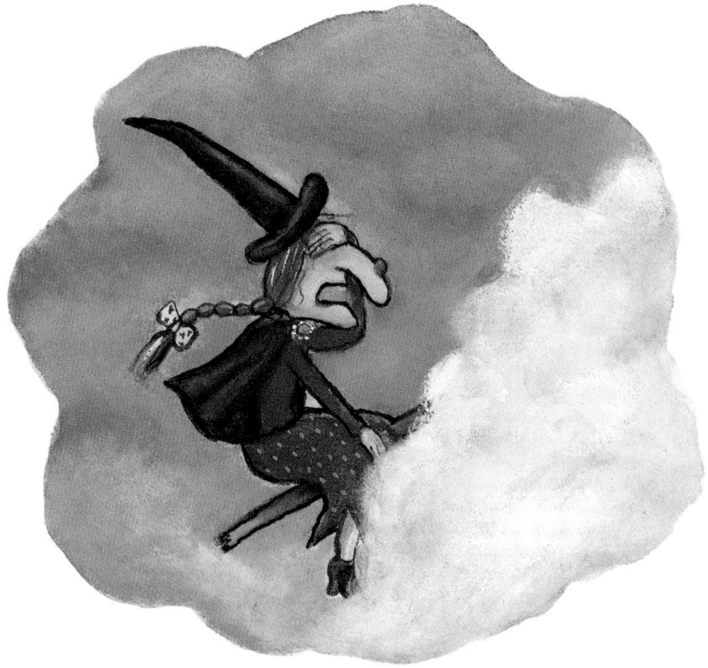

The witch's half-broomstick
flew into a cloud,
And the witch heard a roar
that was scary and loud . . .

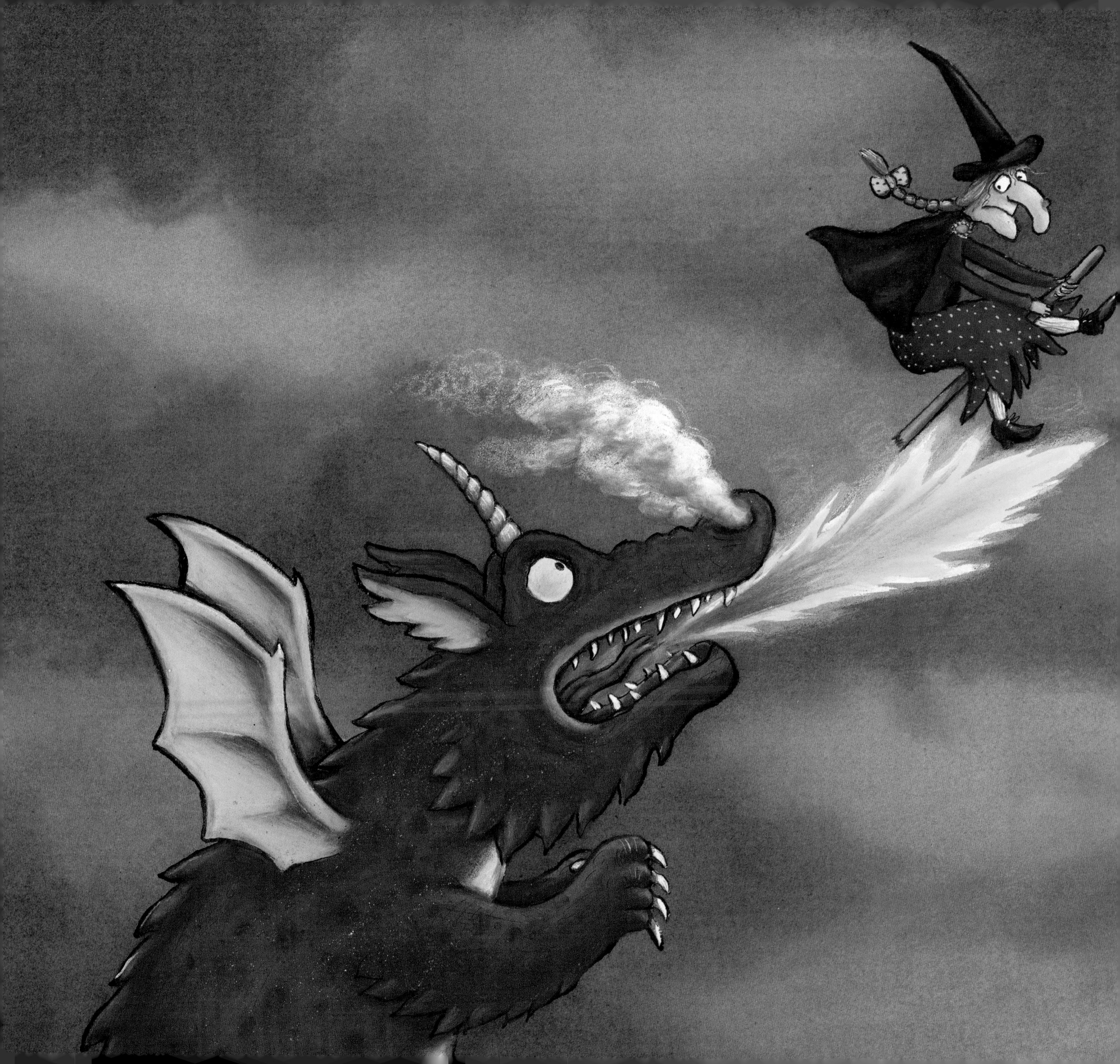

"I am a dragon, as mean as can be,
And witch with french fries
tastes delicious to me!"
"No!" cried the witch,
flying higher and higher.
The dragon flew after her,
breathing out fire.
"Help!" cried the witch,
flying down to the ground.
She looked all around
but no help could be found.

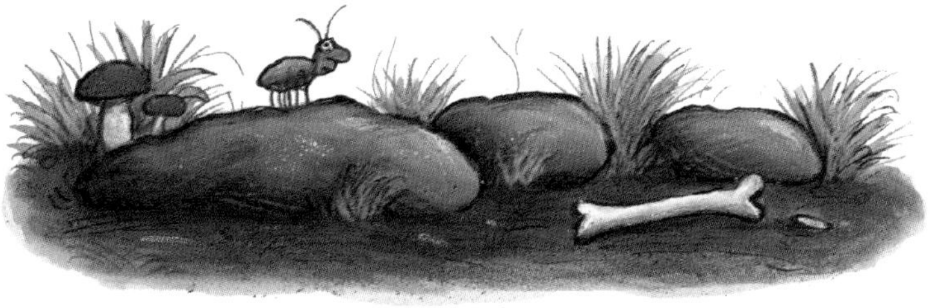

The dragon drew near
with a glint in his eyes,
And said, "Just this once
I'll have witch without fries."

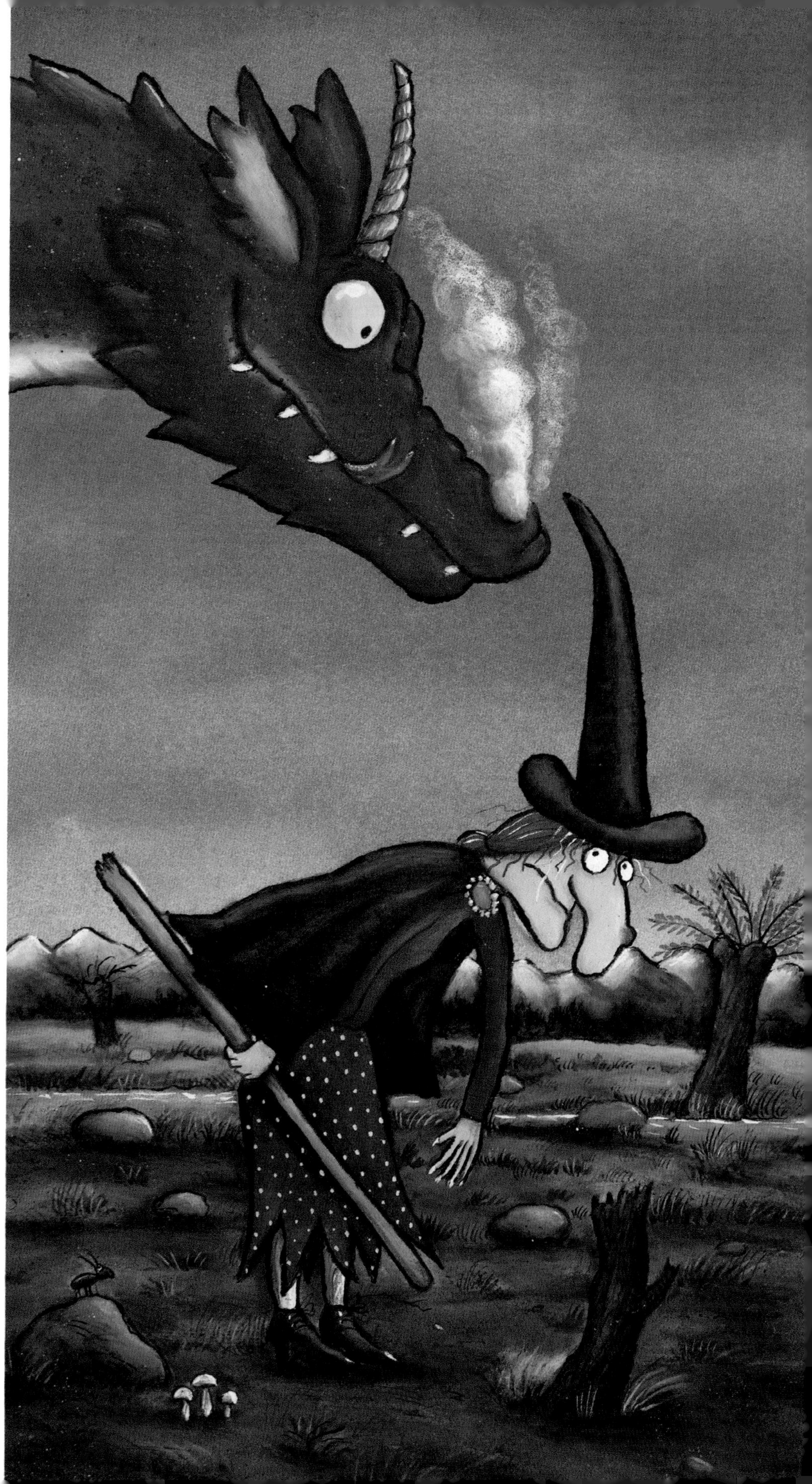

B ut just as he planned
    to begin on his feast,
From out of a ditch
    rose a horrible beast.
It was tall, dark, and sticky,
    and feathered and furred.
It had four frightful heads,
    it had wings like a bird.
And its terrible voice,
    when it started to speak,
Was a yowl and a growl
    and a croak and a shriek.
It dripped and it squelched
    as it strode from the ditch,
And it said to the dragon,
    "Buzz off!—
    THAT'S MY WITCH!"

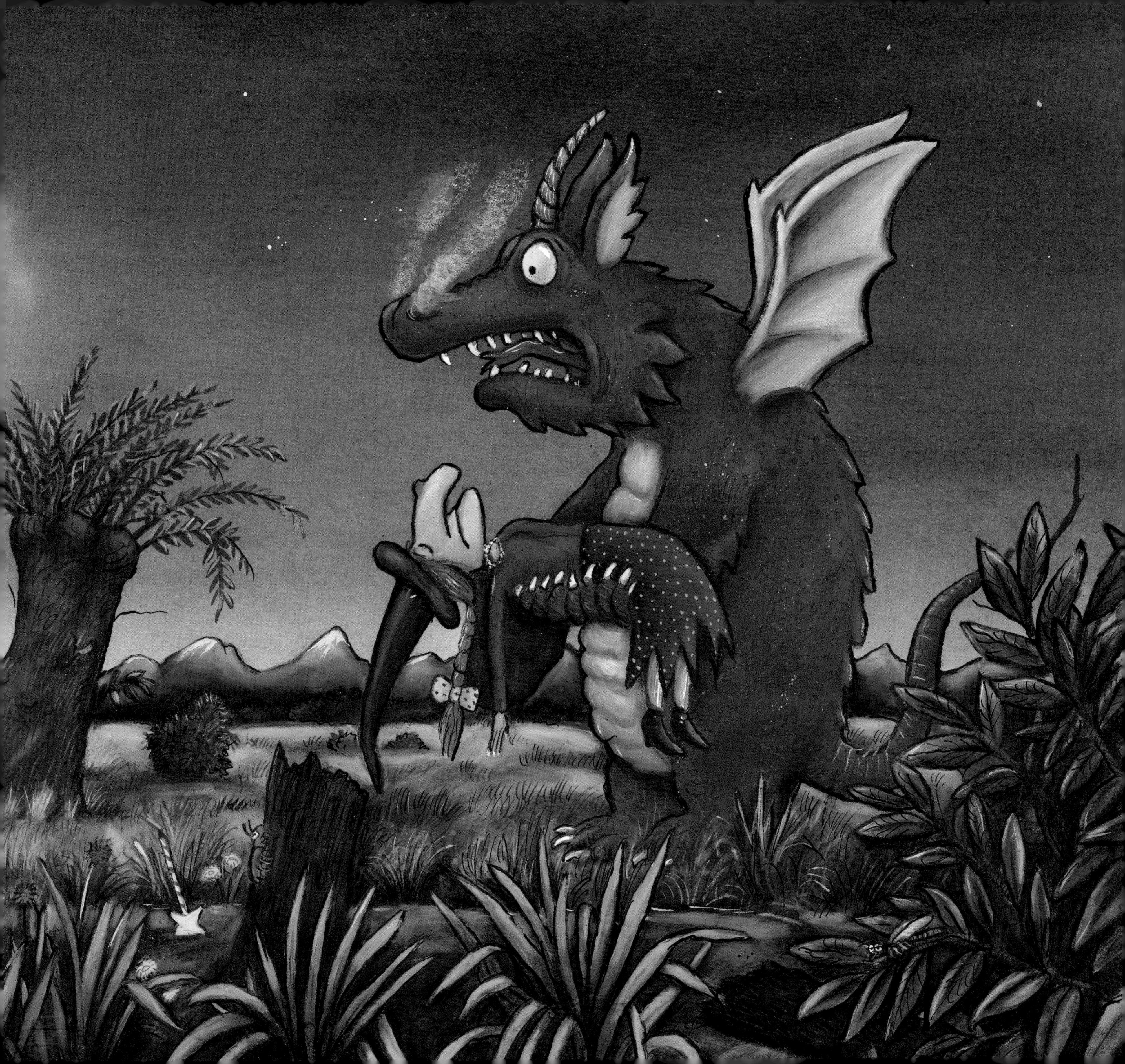

The dragon drew back
   and he started to shake.
"I'm sorry!" he spluttered.
   "I made a mistake.
It's nice to have met you,
   but now I must fly."
And he spread out his wings
   and was off through the sky.

Then down flew the bird
   and down jumped the frog.
Down climbed the cat,
   and, "Phew!" said the dog.
And, "Thank you, oh, thank you!"
   the grateful witch cried.
"Without you I'd be
   in that dragon's inside."

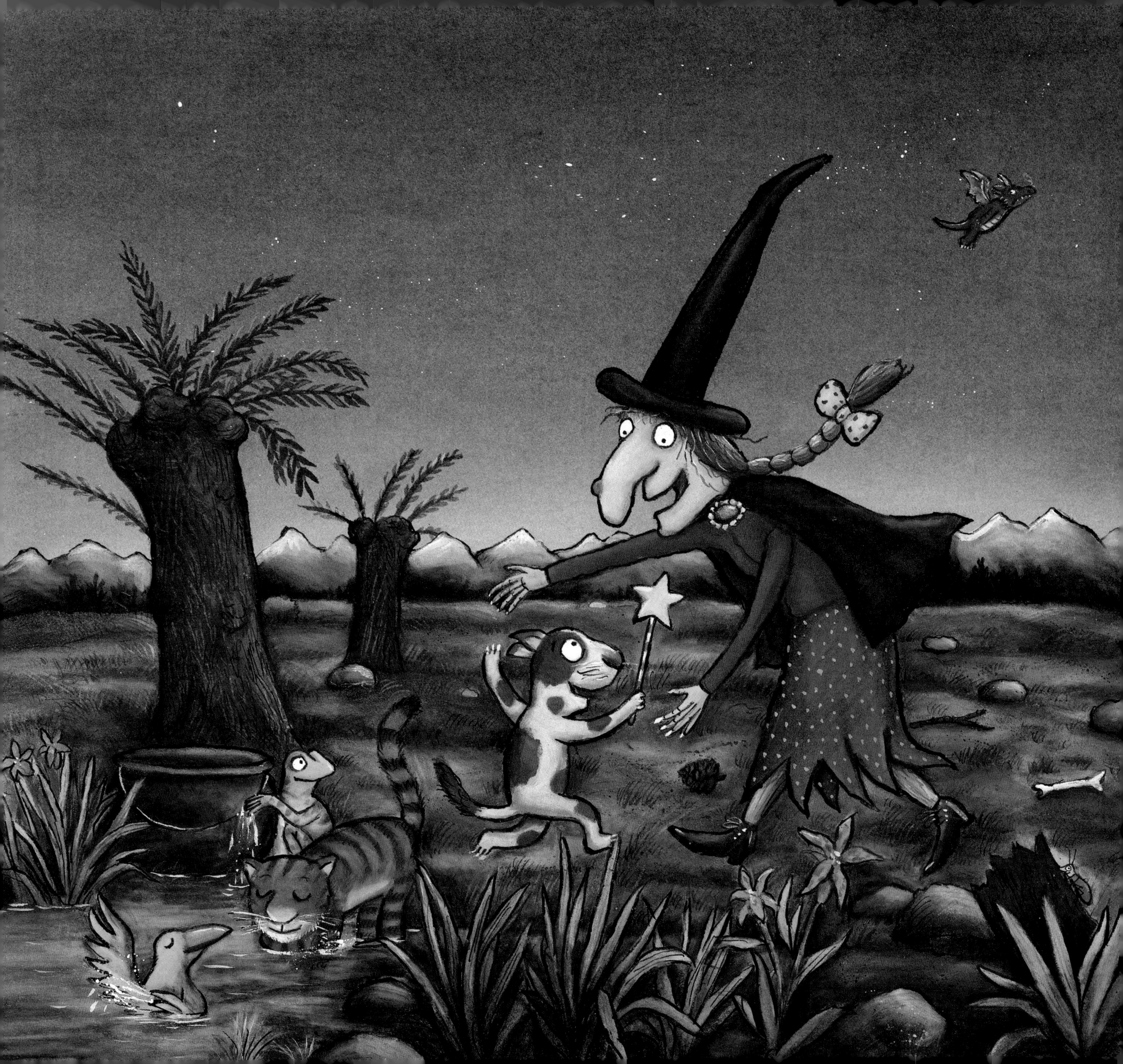

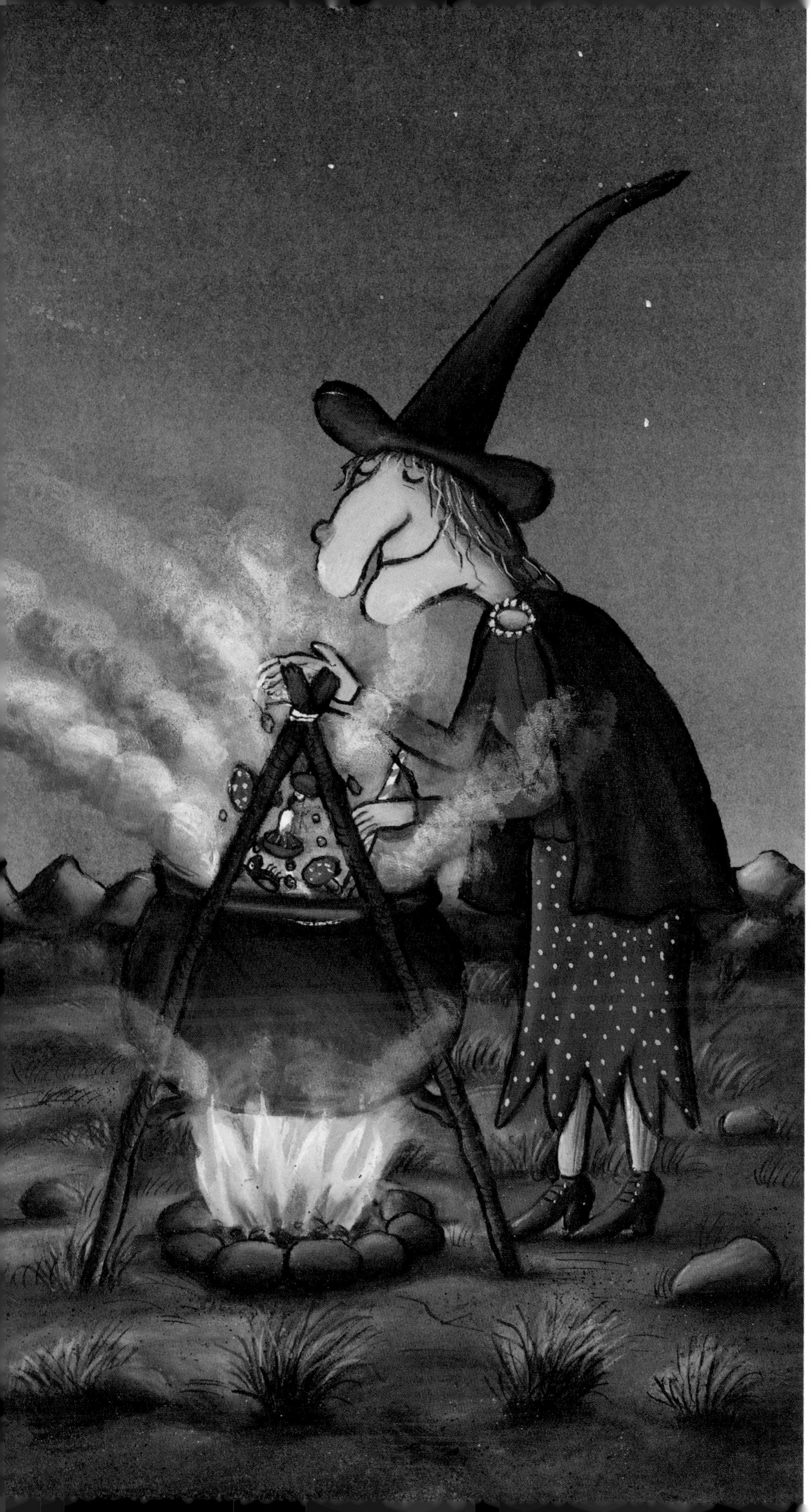

Then she filled up her cauldron
and said with a grin,
"Find something, everyone,
throw something in!"
So the frog found a lily,
the cat found a cone,
The bird found a twig,
and the dog found a bone.

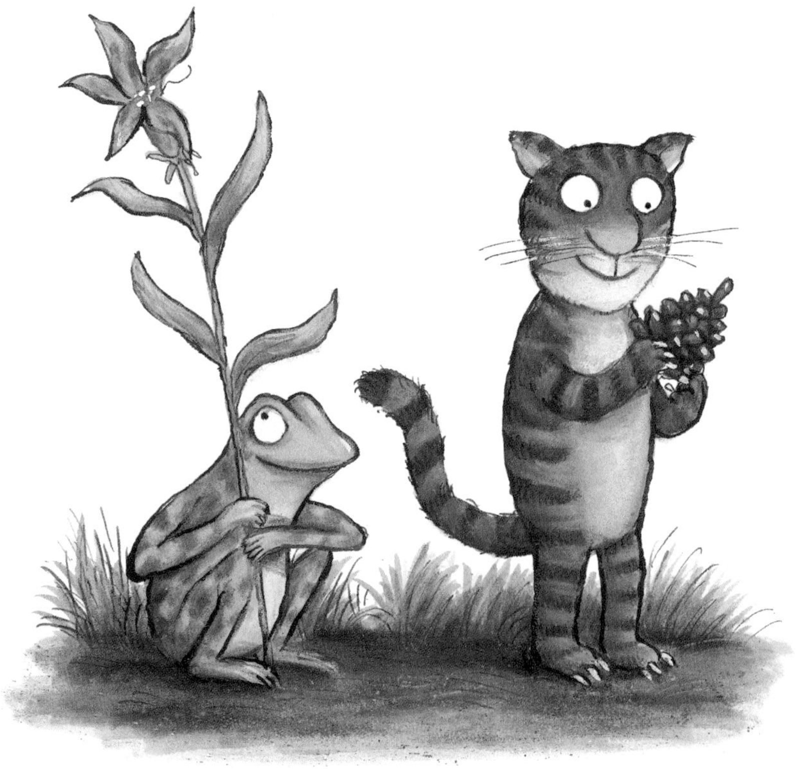

They threw them all in
and the witch stirred them well,
And while she was stirring,
she muttered a spell.
"Iggety, ziggety, zaggety, ZOOM!"

Then out rose . . .

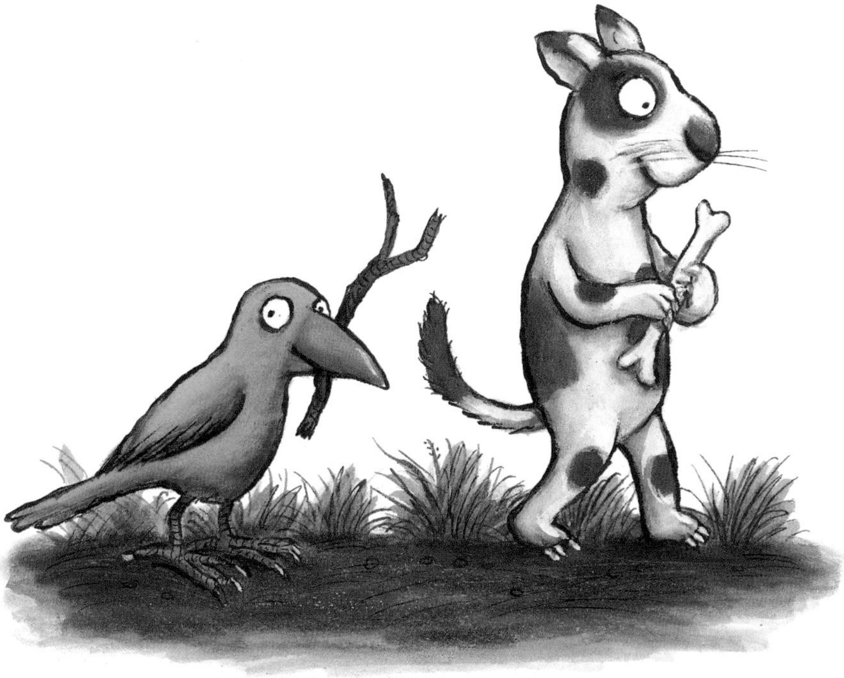

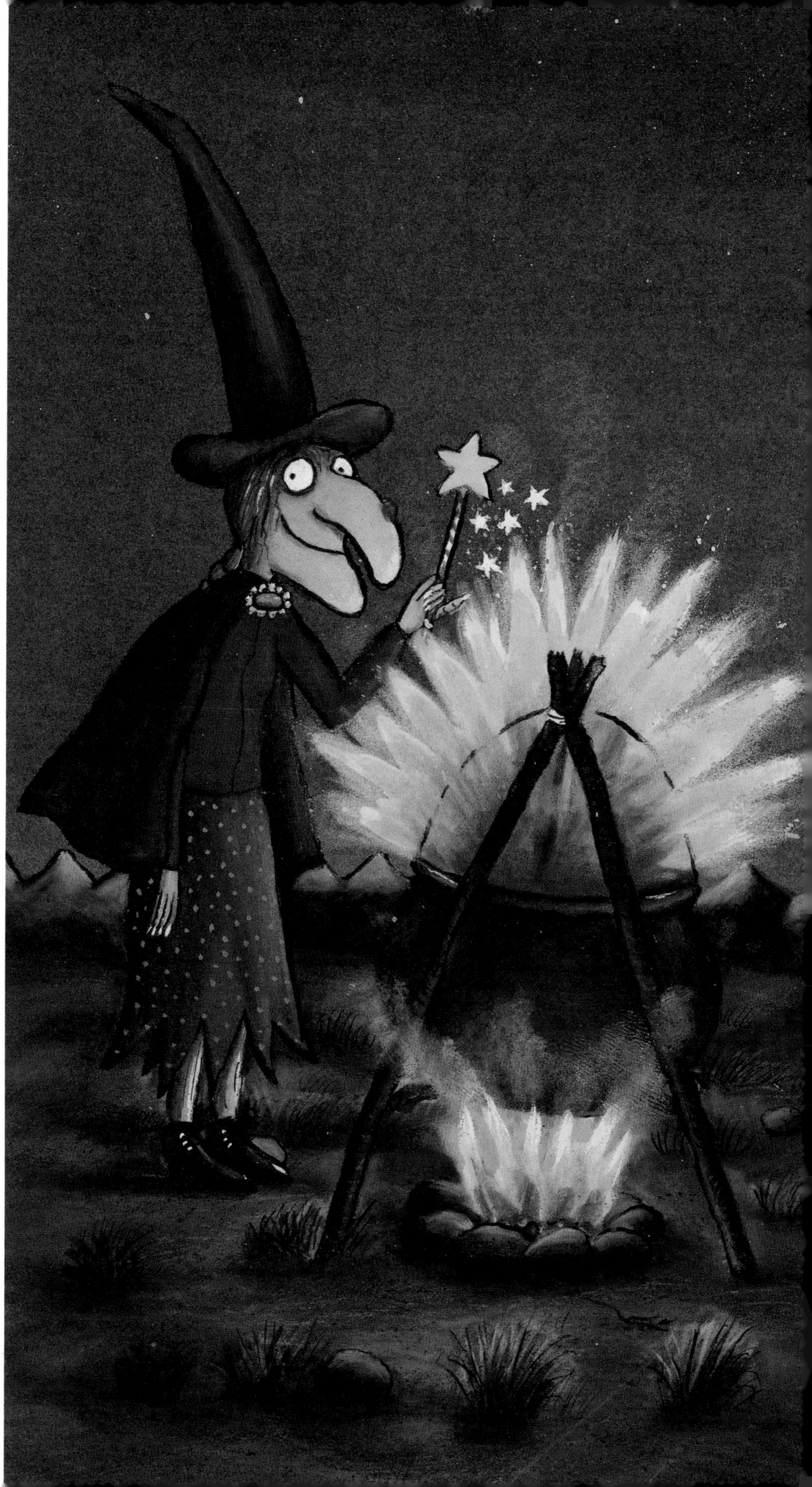

A TRULY MAGNIFICENT BROOM!

With seats for the witch
and the cat and the dog,
A nest for the bird and
a pool for the frog.

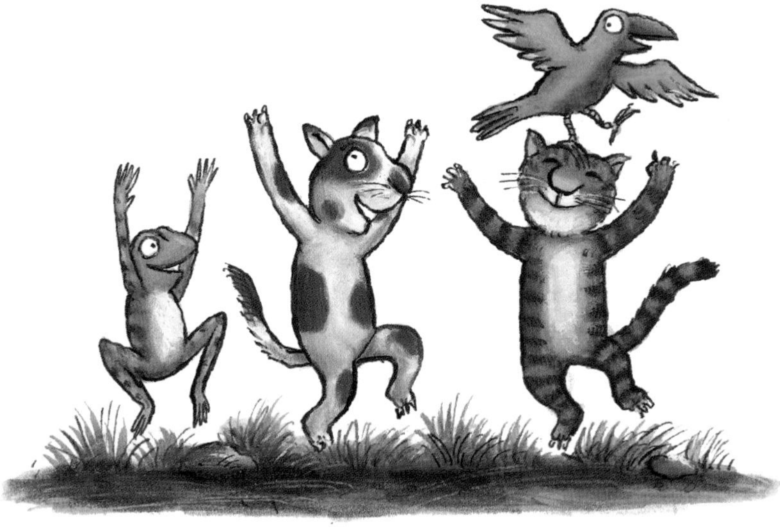

"Yes!" cried the witch,
and they all clambered on.
The witch tapped the broomstick and
whoosh! they were gone.

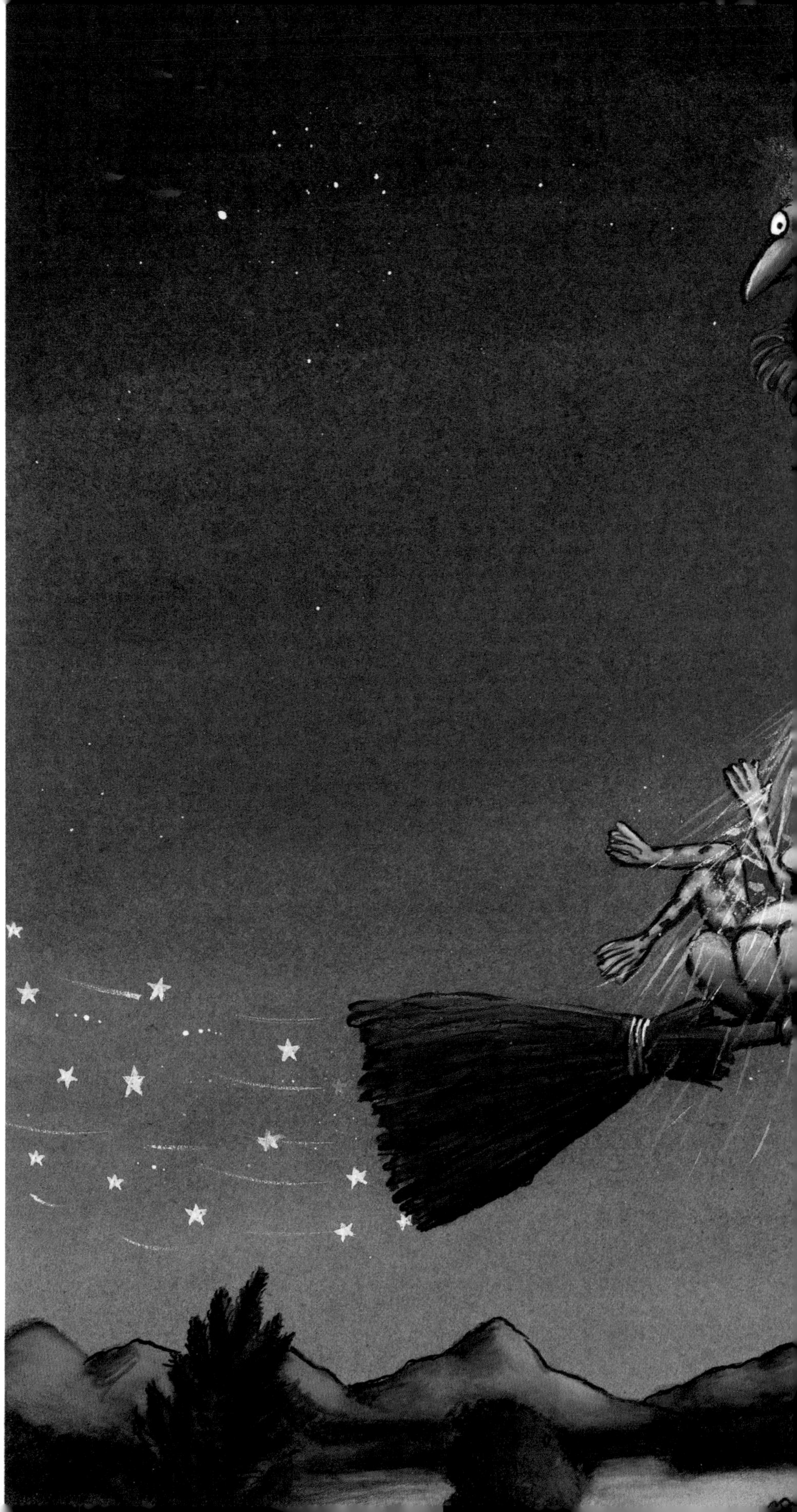

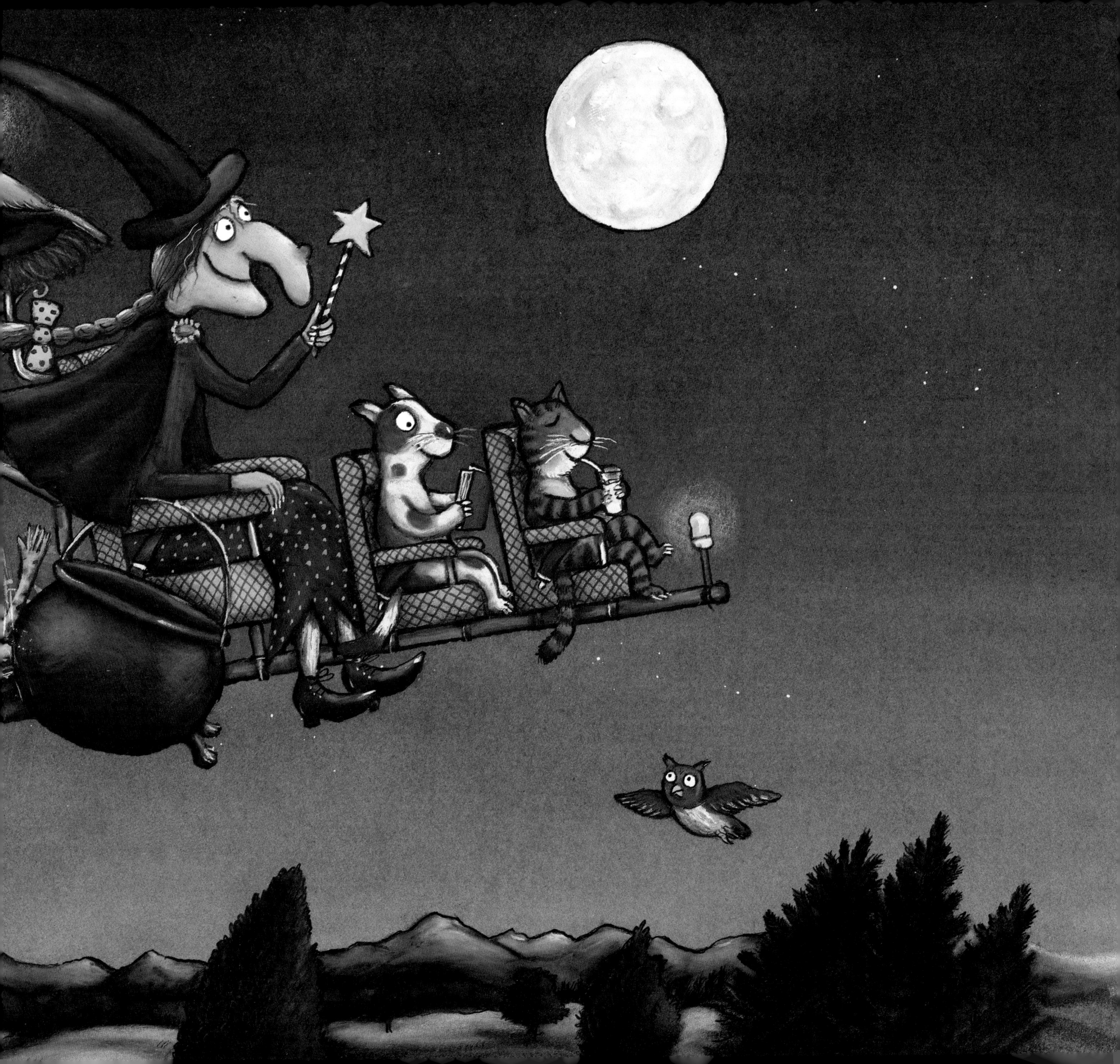

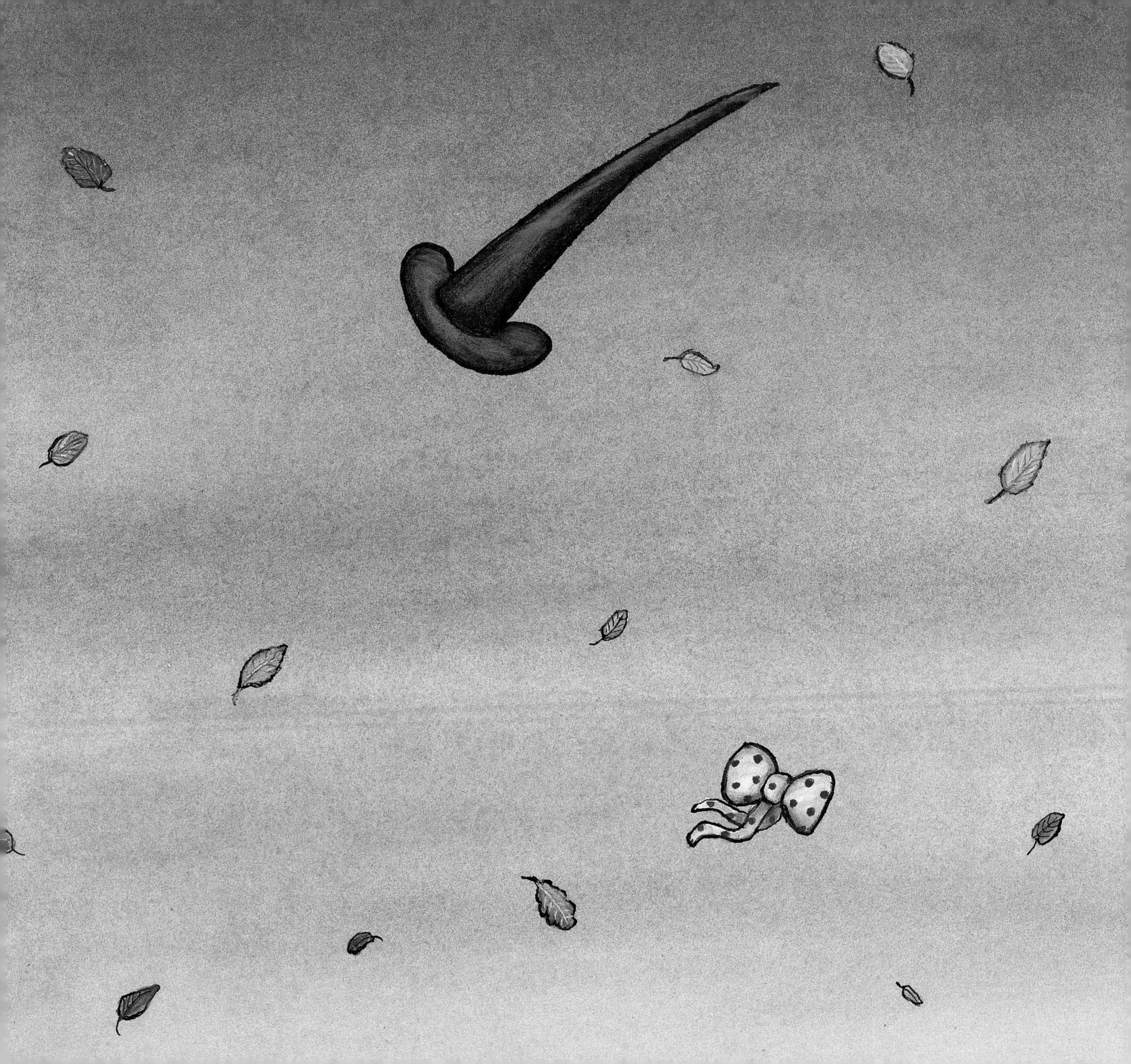

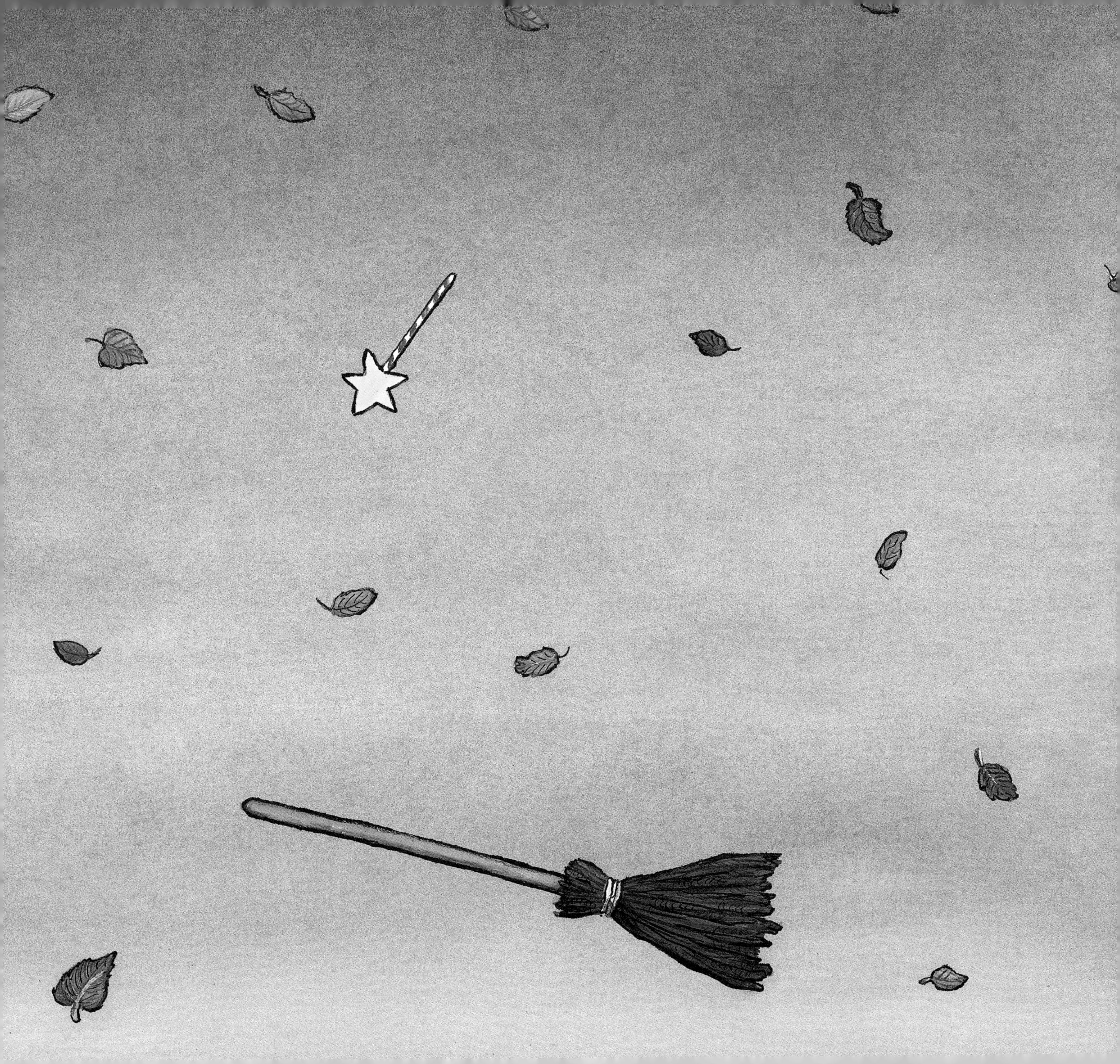

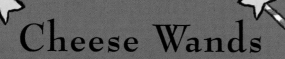

Cheese Wands

Have fun making these twisty cheese wands.
They're so delicious that you and your friends
will make them disappear in a flash!

Before you start, make sure you . . .

★ Have a grown-up with you at all times.

★ Wash your hands so they're nice and clean.
You'll need to wash them again at the end, too.

★ Put on an apron and tie your hair back if it's long.

★ Read the recipe with your grown-up to make sure
you have everything you need.

★ Be very careful around anything hot or sharp.

You will need:

★ 1 cup plain flour

★ ¼ cup butter (cubed)

★ ¼ cup cheddar cheese (grated)

★ 1 egg (beaten)

★ Extra flour for dusting

★ Cooking spray, oil, or butter
for greasing

★ A baking tray

★ A large mixing bowl

★ A small star-shaped cutter

★ A rolling pin

★ A butter knife

★ A pastry brush

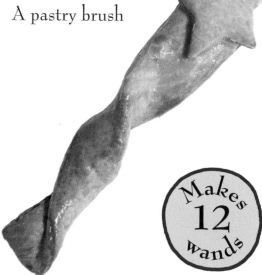

Makes
12
wands